If You Decide
to Go to the
moon

By **FAITH MCNULTY**

Illustrated by **STEVEN KELLOGG**

If you decide to go to the moon
in your own rocket ship,
read this book before you start.

It will tell you how to get there
and what to do after you land.
The most important part tells
you how to get home.

Check the things you will need:
space suit, air tanks, books, and games.
Don't forget your diary and plenty of food.
Peanut butter, apples, and cake
will taste good in space.
Water and juice are also important.

To get to the moon, you will travel
about 240,000 miles—
a long trip, but rocket ships go fast.
If you average 3,750 miles per hour,
you will get there in two-and-a-half days.

STOP
ASTRONAUTS ONLY
BEYOND THIS POINT

Get aboard. Close the hatch. Light the burners.

TEN

NINE

EIGHT

SEVEN

SIX

FIVE

FOUR

THREE

TWO

ONE

BLAST OFF!

You shoot up . . . up . . . up into the sky.
As your ship rises through the clouds,
your body is pressed against the seat.
At first you feel very heavy. Don't worry.
This feeling will go away.

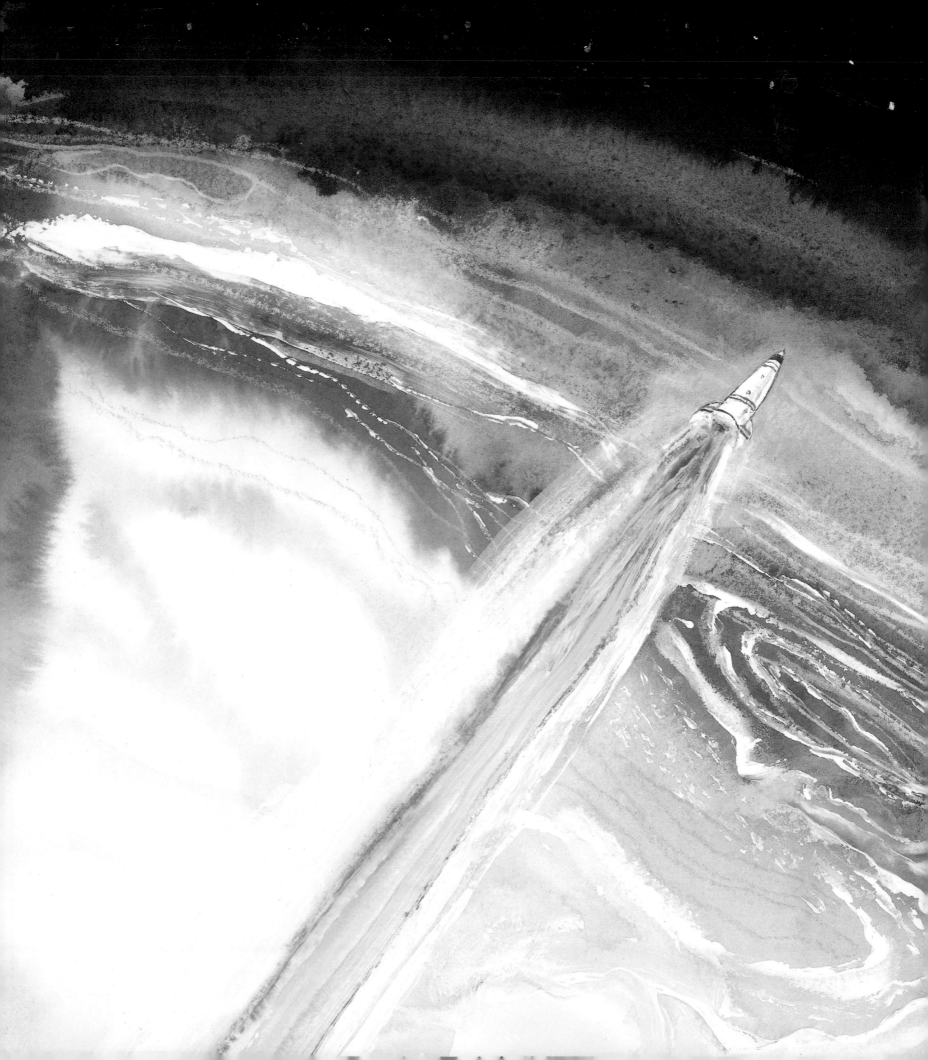

For a few seconds you fly
through a mixture of clouds and air
and dust that hangs over the earth.
It is not very thick—only about fifteen miles.
You will shoot right through it into space.

Space is dark and empty. . . .
There is no air in space; no clouds; no rain;
only a few specks of dust,
some rocks called meteors,
and some chunks of ice called comets.
Both meteors and comets are pieces of stars
that exploded long ago and have been
flying around in space ever since.
If one hit you, it would be very bad,
but space is so big and you are so small
that a collision is unlikely.
In the blackness of space
the stars shine like a million fireflies.

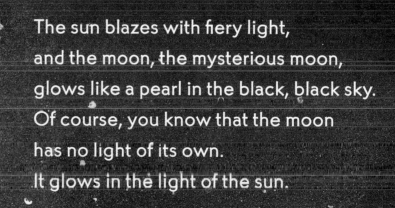

The sun blazes with fiery light,
and the moon, the mysterious moon,
glows like a pearl in the black, black sky.
Of course, you know that the moon
has no light of its own.
It glows in the light of the sun.

Up here in space
you may feel very alone.
Don't look back at the Earth.
It would make you even lonelier.
This is the time to play some cheerful music,
eat a peanut butter sandwich,
keep your eyes fixed on the shining moon,
and settle down for a long ride.

Relax. Take off your seat belt and
be prepared for a surprise.
Because you are weightless in space,
you'll feel amazingly light.
You will float like a feather
inside the cabin and bounce
off the cabin walls.
But you'll bounce very lightly
and find it a lot of fun.

When you are thirsty, don't try to pour
orange juice into a glass.
With everything weightless,
it would collect into floating liquid balls
and become an orange juice blob.
You can drink out of a squeeze bottle instead.
After supper and a squeeze of juice,
it's time for bed.

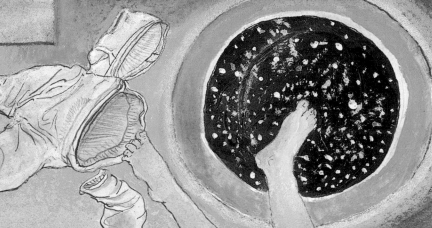

Tie yourself to your bunk so you won't float away,
and settle down for a good night's sleep.
Of course, there is no night in space.
You will have to pretend.
Try to have sweet dreams.

When you wake you will be much closer to the moon.
It will be big and round and very bright
with dark patches that look like lakes or seas.
They were made billions of years ago
when the moon was very hot,
hot enough to melt stone.

Now and then, melted stone
spurted up through the crust
and spread out on the surface
like spilled soup.
When it cooled, it hardened
into stone, called lava.
From Earth, these smooth,
dark places look like oceans.

Playing cards will help to pass the time,
but if you drop them they will drift
around the cabin like butterflies.
Floating around to catch them
feels like swimming in a dream.

The first humans to go to the moon
landed on the Sea of Tranquility.
It is marked on your moon map
and would be a good place to land.

But you still have a long way to go.
When you are tired, lie down
and look at all the stars.
On Earth you see only the stars that are above you.
Up here there are stars in every direction.
You might write in your diary:
"I wonder how far space goes and where it ends?"

At last, when you have read all your books
and played all your games,
you wake from a nap
and see the moon right there below you.
You look down on an endless desert.
Everything is all one color—silvery gray.
The ground is covered with rocks and round craters.
Craters are holes made by meteors that have
rained down on the moon through the ages.
Some were huge and made deep holes
hundreds of miles across.
Of course, you steer clear of the rocky places.

At last you see
a lava lake below—
the Sea of Tranquility.
Get ready to land!
As you descend,
your craft shivers and shakes.
It settles softly.
You feel a bump.

YOU ARE ON THE MOON!

Your first look will be disappointing.
All you see through your porthole
is a cloud of dust stirred up by your landing.
Put on your space suit and air tank while
you wait for it to settle.
Then open the hatch and jump out.

You will land lightly.
The moon is smaller than
the Earth and has less gravity
to pull you down.
If you weigh sixty pounds on Earth,
you will weigh only ten on the moon.

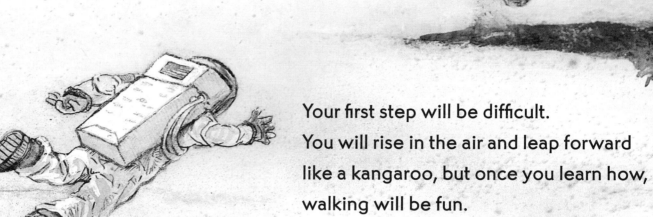

Your first step will be difficult.
You will rise in the air and leap forward
like a kangaroo, but once you learn how,
walking will be fun.

Each step takes you five times as far
as a step on Earth.
Leaping over boulders and craters,
you cover the ground with magical swiftness.
The moonscape is strange,
but it doesn't look dangerous.
The dust reminds you of cake flour.
You wish you could take off your suit
and play in it.

DON'T DO IT!

The heat of the sun would burn you up!

Because there is no air or water on the moon,
there are no clouds to shield it from the heat
of the sun, or the cold of space.
Anything touched by the sun is blistering hot.
Anything in shadow is instantly cold.
Without a space suit, you would sizzle or freeze.

As you walk, you will notice that

your boots don't crunch on the pebbles.

If you take a hammer and hit a rock,

there is no bang.

It is impossible to make a noise on the moon.

Without air to carry sound waves,

you can't hear a bell ring, you can't hear a horn blow.

You can't hear a whistle or a song on the moon.

If you kick a pebble, it will bounce without a sound.

As you keep walking,
the silence and stillness are eerie.
Nothing moves.
The boulders and hills have strange shapes.
Some hills look like dinosaurs;
some boulders look like giant turtles,
or weird birds, or a herd of cows.
A heap of jagged rocks looks like a ruined castle.
You feel as if you might be in a fairy tale.
Or is it a dream?

Your map tells you that the
astronauts' camp is just over the next hill.
As you climb you wonder
if things will look different on the other side.
Will you find something green?
Something alive? A meadow of moongrass?
A herd of mooncows?

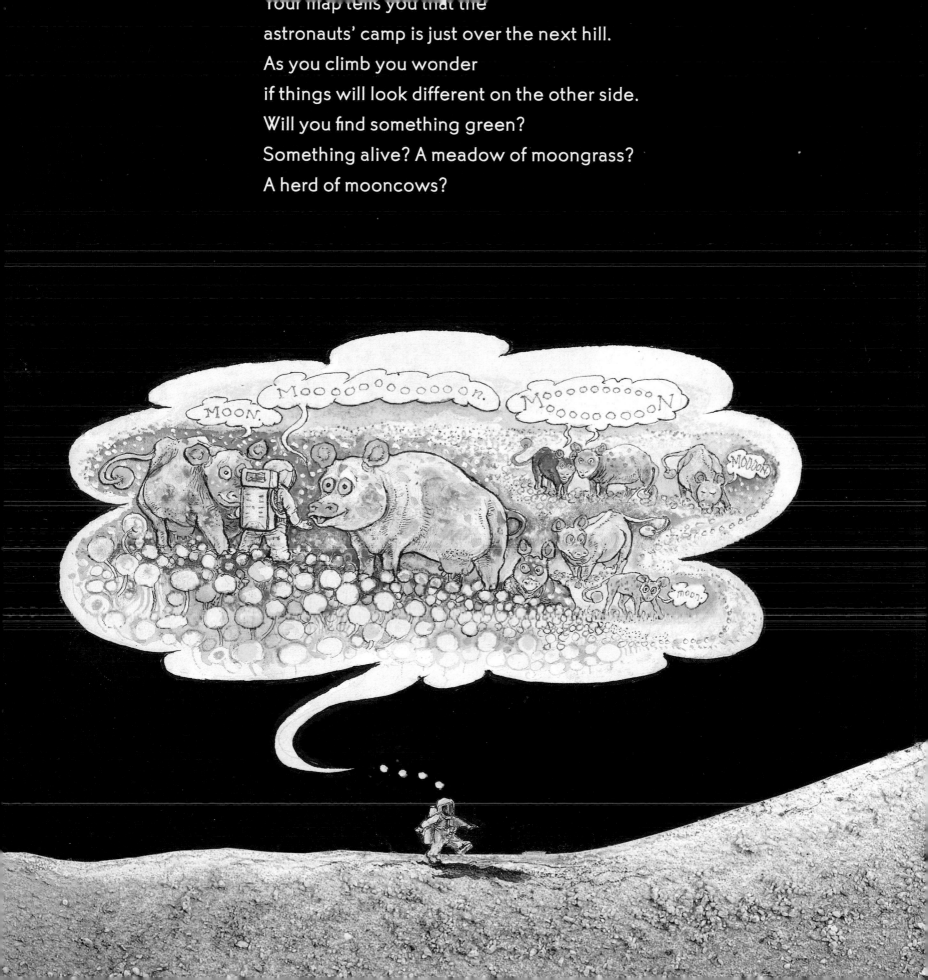

The answer is "no."

The hills stretch on and on
to the horizon, where the rim of the moon
meets the blackness of space.
Everything on the moon is lifeless and still.

use your binoculars to scan the distance.
Look for a patch of color—the red, white, and blue
of the flag that the astronauts left behind.
It will stand out against the gray dust.

As you get close to the camp,
you will see everything the astronauts
left behind. Strewn amidst the lunar dust,
tools and equipment are scattered about.
Their boot prints look fresh,
as though they were made a moment ago.
There is no wind or rain to wear them away.
The astronauts left a message for
anyone who visits the moon.
You find it written on a plaque:
Here men from the planet Earth
first set foot on the moon. July 1969 A.D.

But the flag they planted isn't flying.
The flagpole was blown over from the blast
when the astronauts took off
and the flag is lying in the dust.
You pick it up and push it deep into the sand.
The flag is stiffened with wires so that it looks
as though it is flying even though there is no wind.
It is a brave and wonderful sight and reminds you
of the courage of the astronauts who brought it here.

If astronauts ever return
they will find the flag flying once again,
and your footprints in the dust.

By now your tank of air must be half empty.

It's time to return to your ship.

Your trail of footprints will lead you back.

You retrace your steps in leaps and bounds.

When you see your spaceship waiting,

you are suddenly terribly homesick.

You can't wait to get back to Earth. . . .

Take a last look at the moonscape.

Get aboard. Close the hatch

and pray that the computers will start.

You push buttons.
Lights flicker. Machinery whirs.
Rockets fire. Your ship lifts off.
Your heart lifts, too,
but you have thousands of miles
to travel. You'll just have to be patient.

Whenever you feel discouraged,
look through your porthole.
You will see a beautiful sight—
Earth, surrounded by stars,
shining like a blue-and-white ball
on a Christmas tree.

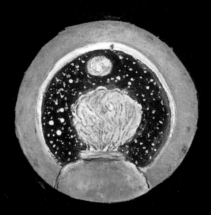

The nearer you get to Earth,
the more wonderful Earth will seem.
Finally, you are close enough to see
the continents and the oceans.
You can see clouds and rain and wind
moving across them, connecting
everything on Earth.

Your trip is almost over.
Your ship has reached the atmosphere.
You drop down through clouds
and land on green grass.

You jump out, thankful for
a miraculous journey and a safe return.

As you bend down to kiss the ground,
you promise you will always do your best
to protect all life on our beautiful Earth.

To Katherine White

—F. M.

To Bailey with love

—S. K.

Sincere thanks to Dr. Neil de Grasse Tyson, Director of the Hayden Planetarium, New York City